Greater Tuna

by Jaston Williams
Joe Sears
Ed Howard

SAMUEL FRENCH, INC.

45 West 25th Street   **NEW YORK 10010**
7623 Sunset Boulevard   **HOLLYWOOD 90046**
LONDON   *TORONTO*

PS 3573 .I449327 G7 1983

Williams, Jaston.

Greater Tuna

IMPORTANT ADVERTISING NOTE

All producers of GREATER TUNA shall announce the names of the authors. Jaston Williams, Joe Sears and Ed Howard shall receive billing as sole authors of the Work in any and all advertising and publicity issued in connection with your production hereunder. The billing of the authors shall appear in but not be limited to all theatre programs, houseboards, throwaways, circulars, announcements, and whenever and wherever the title of the Work appears and shall be on separate lines upon which no other matter appears, immediately following the title of the Work. The names of the authors shall be in size, type and prominence at least fifty (50%) percent of the size, type and prominence of the title type or the type accorded to the names of the stars, whichever is larger. The billing shall be in the following form:

(Name of Producer)

presents

Greater Tuna

by

JASTON WILLIAMS
JOE SEARS
ED HOWARD

GREATER TUNA by Jaston Williams, Joe Sears, and Ed Howard opened in New York City, on October 21, 1982, at Circle in the Square Downtown. It was produced by Karl Allison in association with Bryan Bantry, directed by Ed Howard, set by Kevin Rupnik, lights by Judy Rasmuson, costumes by Linda Fisher. The Production Stage Manager was Marjorie Horne; General Manager, The Kingwill Office; Company Manager, Susan Sampliner.

The cast was:

JOE SEARS as	JASTON WILLIAMS as
Thurston Wheelis	Arles Struvie
Elmer Watkins	Didi Snavely
Bertha Bumiller	Harold Dean Lattimer
Yippy	Petey Fisk
Leonard Childers	Jody Bumiller
Pearl Burras	Stanley Bumiller
R. R. Snavely	Charlene Bumiller
Rev. Spikes	Chad Hartford
Sheriff Givens	Phinas Blye
Hank Bumiller	Vera Carp

CIRCLE IN THE SQUARE

(DOWNTOWN) — 159 BLEECKER STREET — 254-6330

KARL ALLISON
in association with BRYAN BANTRY
presents

JOE SEARS   JASTON WILLIAMS

in

Greater TUNA

by

JASTON WILLIAMS   JOE SEARS   ED HOWARD

Scenery by	Costumes by	Lighting by
KEVIN RUPNIK	LINDA FISHER	JUDY RASMUSON

Production Stage Manager	General Management	Associate Producer
MARJORIE HORNE	THE KINGWILL OFFICE	SALISBURY PRODUCTIONS. LTD.

Directed by
ED HOWARD

for Carol Hall

NOTES

GREATER TUNA has been played on an "open", three-sided stage and on a proscenium stage. In the New York production, the audience was on three sides. The various locales were very simply suggested, sometimes with lighting, other times with the simplest set prop, such as a table or a chair. If you wish to produce GREATER TUNA successfully, remember the old dictum: "Less is always better."

Country-western music, in the style of Patsy Cline, is suggested for use throughout the play. Producers are cautioned, though, that permission to produce GREATER TUNA does not automatically include permission to use music which is still under copyright protection.

In the original production of GREATER TUNA, all the denizens of Tuna, Texas, were played by two actors. It is the opinion of the authors that this greatly increases the fun of the show; but it is recognized that individual producers, such as school and community theatre groups, may wish to expand the cast size, perhaps having women play the female roles (maybe even some of the male roles). This issue is left up to the discretion of individual producers.

Greater Tuna

ACT ONE

Opening MUSIC; LIGHTS UP on and inside radio

ON TAPE. (*radio test pattern followed by announcer*) This is Radio Station OKKK in Tuna, Texas, serving the Greater Tuna area at two hundred and seventy-five watts, signing on.

(*LIGHTS UP on Studio*)

THURSTON. Good morning, Tuna, this is Thurston Wheelis.

ARLES. And this is Arles Struvie,

THURSTON. And this is the Wheelis—

ARLES. Struvie—

THURSTON. Report.

ARLES. And here we go with the news. Take it away, Thurston.

THURSTON. Well, folks, in the news today, we've got the winner of the Tuna Junior High American Heritage Essay Contest for this year. And this year's winner is Connie Carp. She's the daughter of W.H. and Vera Carp here in Tuna, and the name of her essay was titled "Human Rights, Why Bother?" Second place went to Jimbo Beaumont for "Living with Radiation", and third place went to Levita Posey for her essay titled, "The Other Side of Bigotry." I'll tell you, Arles, with subjects like that, I don't know how they ever picked a winner.

ARLES. I don't either. I tell you, it should make the citizens of Tuna proud to know that we're still producing well-educated students who know what America is all about.

THURSTON. They do.

ARLES. They do. They do. They do.

THURSTON. (*overlap*) They do. I always thought they did a fine job.	ARLES. (*overlap*) Thank you Ronnie. This just in.

ARLES. Excuse me, Thurston.

THURSTON. Go right ahead.

ARLES. Oh, I have bad news for the Greater Tuna area. Former County Judge Roscoe Buckner died at his home yesterday; he had suffered a severe stroke. Buckner, who was judge in the Greater Tuna area for forty-seven years and who hung more people in the thirties than any other active judge, had a history of heart trouble. Now, the body will lie in state at Hubert Funeral Home, starting today at twelve noon, and Wexler Hubert says if you come before noon you're gonna have to wait, 'cause the Judge won't be ready till noon.

THURSTON. Well, I tell ya, folks, that's some bad news.

ARLES. It is.

THURSTON. It is.

ARLES. It is. It is. Now, on the Art scene, the on-again, off-again auditions for the Tuna Little Theatre production of "My Fair Lady" are on again. Now, they'd been called off due to a lack of budget. But Joe Bob Lipsey, who is the director of the show this year, and who is a recent graduate of Southwest Texas Eastern A and I State University, said that he found a way to go ahead with the production by using sets and costumes from last year's show of "South Pacific." And according to Joe Bob, this is gonna be the first production ever of "My Fair Lady" set in Polynesia.

THURSTON. Well, Arles, you never know, something like that's just li'ble to put us on the map.

ARLES. On it.

ARLES. (*overlap*) On it.   THURSTON. (*overlap*) On it. On it.   On it.

THURSTON. They'll find us.

ARLES. So Joe Bob says get on your Hawaiian shirts, and your grass skirts, and your coconuts, and get out there to that Coweta Baptist Church at eight-thirty, Thursday night, and audition for "My Fair Lady." And Joe Bob says he wants to integrate the cast this year. So if you know of any Negro or Mexican-American actors or actresses, have 'em come on out and try out for the chorus.

THURSTON. That's right. Come on out.

ARLES. Come on out.

THURSTON. Come on out. You never know, you just might get a part.

ARLES. You might. You might. Well, Thurston, you got that farm report? (*ARLES exits and changes to DIDI.*)

THURSTON. Oh, yeah, I got that farm report . . . Well, folks, it's goin' to be an incomplete farm report, because not everything is in just yet — but I got beef up, pork down, chickens vascillatin', and uh, I don't know that much about sowbellies . . . But I do know it's time for a word from our sponsor, Didi Snavely of Didi's Used Weapons. And here's Didi now to tell us all about it. Didi. (*DIDI enters.*)

DIDI. Does the high cost of security have you blue? If so, come by the store and browse through our complete selection of used guns and knives, or find what you need in our mace and tear gas department. Now we understand that many people are hesitant to buy used weapons, but all of Didi's weapons are absolutely guaranteed to kill. Now if you find a weapon here that won't kill, you bring it back and we'll give you something that will. It's on our guarantee: "If Didi's can't kill it, it's immortal." (*DIDI exits and changes to HAROLD DEAN.*)

THURSTON. Thank you Didi. It's always a pleasure to have Didi here with us. Thank you Didi, and now for that weather report, we're gonna go out there to the field with Harold Dean Lattimer. Harold Dean, what's it gonna be? (*HAROLD DEAN enters.*)

HAROLD DEAN. Well, it's gonna be a little bit of everything. We're expecting a lot of rain from the East and the West and the North, and a little bit from the South. But by mid-morning, it will have cleared off, and by noon it should be unbearably hot and humid. We're expecting about a hundred, a hundred-and-one. Now for the afternoon, we got some possible dust storms from out in West Texas. They could be severe. They say the sky could go completely black around four o'clock in the afternoon. Now we also have this swarm of locusts that are headin' our way from Louisiana but we figure the dust will kill a lot of 'em, and the rest'll probably get blown away or drown in this tropical storm that's headin' our way from the coast, and that'll be tropical storm Luther. And that storm's gonna hit here about 10 o'clock. It'll bring a lot of rain with it. It's gonna be wet, and cloudy, and miserable, and it's gonna rain . . . for several days. So get out those raincoats. Back to you, Thurston. (*HAROLD DEAN exits and changes to ARLES.*)

THURSTON. Well, you heard it, folks, rain. You know, Harold Dean has to get up every morning about 4:30 to give these weather reports. Sometimes we'll be drivin' to the studio and we'll look out there in the field and see him standin' there in God-only-knows what kind of weather. (*ARLES enters.*)

ARLES. Hell, I've seen him up to his neck in snow before.

THURSTON. 'Member that time he spotted that water spout over Bumiller's Pond?

ARLES. Picked him up and dropped him in Dewey County.

THURSTON. And he still got that report in on time.

ARLES. He did.

THURSTON. He did.

ARLES. (*overlap*) He   THURSTON. (*overlap*)
did. He did.   Damn sure did.

ARLES. Thank you, Ronnie. This just in . . . A U.F.O., that is an unidentified flying object, has been spotted by R.R. Snavely, over Lake Mobete. R.R. says it looks like a gigantic hovering chalupa without the guacamole.

ARLES. Well, that's what it says.

THURSTON. (*overlap*)   ARLES. (*overlap*)
It does.   It does.

ARLES. It does. It does. And from our World News Desk: Peace talks fail, attack is imminent.

THURSTON. Ummm.

ARLES. Well, that's all the news we got for ya, but stay tuned.

THURSTON. Stay tuned.

ARLES. 'Cause we got Leonard on the Line comin' up . . .

THURSTON. (*interrupting*) Oh. Thank you Ronnie.

Gotta note here. "You forgot to throw the power switch. You are not on the air."

ARLES. Gahhhh!

THURSTON. (*throws switch*) Good morning, Tuna. This is Thurston Wheelis.

ARLES. And this is Arles Struvie.

THURSTON. And this is the Wheelis.

ARLES. Struvie . . .

(*MUSIC. They exit. THURSTON changes to ELMER. ARLES changes to PETEY. ELMER enters.*)

ELMER. This is Elmer Watkins on Station OKKK for Klan 249. I just wanna remind everybody we're gonna have a meetin' tonight down at the meetin' house. We're gonna talk about them sharecroppers down by Hog Shooter Creek. They been takin' up more'n their share of the land down there. And they ain't been leavin' nuthin' for the wild game to live in. And come this fall, there ain't gonna be nuthin' to kill, and that sport's gonna be gone. So I want everybody to show up tonight so we can plan out what we're gonna say to 'em. And I think they're gonna listen. This is Elmer Watkins for Klan 249. Thank you. (*ELMER exits and changes to BERTHA. PETEY enters.*)

PETEY. This is Petey Fisk speaking to you for the Greater Tuna Humane Society, and I would like to ask each of you to take a minute to think about ducks. It's tough being a duck. Cartoons portray ducks as genetic mutants with speech impediments. The very word "duck" when used as a verb means to rapidly lower body position to avoid injury. So when you say "duck" to somebody, they don't know whether you're talking about a bird or an accident . . . and the Chinese eat their feet. Now, you may not know it, but we have a duck-crisis situation right here in Tuna. Ever since the government flooded Buckner Basin, the wild ducks have got no nesting grounds left. We're up to our necks in homeless ducks. To remedy this situation, the Humane Society has published a pamphlet "Duck Trapping Without Trauma," and we're sending copies to every home in the Tuna area. Now you bring the trapped ducks to me, Petey Fisk, and I will personally relocate them in unflooded areas. This is Petey Fisk speaking to you for the Greater Tuna Humane Society. Thank you.

(*MUSIC is heard from the radio. PETEY exits and changes to JODY.*)

BERTHA. (*offstage*) Charlene! Stanley! Don't make me call you again. (*BERTHA enters and turns off radio.*) Jody, honey. Get in here and finish your breakfast. (*JODY enters.*) Jody, honey, you want some more oatmeal?

JODY. No, Mama.

BERTHA. How 'bout some of these biscuits and gravy, honey; you hardly even touched 'em.

JODY. I already had some, Mama.

BERTHA. Well, baby, I could fry you some more bacon.

JODY. Mama, I don't want nothin'.

BERTHA. Is there something wrong with them hash-browns?

JODY. No, Mama.

BERTHA. Well, have some more—Jody, what's that out there on the back porch? Oh, no! No, Jody, you didn't. Uh-uh! I will not have another puppy!

JODY. Mama, it followed me home.

BERTHA. From where?

JODY. From Petey Fisk's.

BERTHA. That Petey Fisk has given you another dog. He saves the dogs of the world and sends them home for me to feed. Well, you can't have another dog. Eight dogs is too many. You cannot have another dog, Little Jody.

JODY. I'll take care of it, Mama.

BERTHA. Honey, it's not a matter of takin' care of it. It's not normal. It's not normal for you to have eight to ten dogs followin' you all the time, and don't let that dog in the house. That reporter from Houston will be here any minute. (*JODY exits and changes to STANLEY.*) I said, don't let that . . . now isn't that the cutest little thing . . . Awwoohhh, get down. Quit. Stop it . . . He's done it to me again. He has done it to me again. Come on, you. Yes, you . . . Come on and get out there with the rest of 'em. I gotta set for an interview. (*to the other dogs*) Get away from that door! All of you! Get back! (*She lets the dog out.*) Now come on, you. You sweet thing. Now y'all let her alone. Bless her heart, isn't she cute? . . . I could kill that God-damned Petey Fisk! (*STANLEY enters.*) Stanley, honey, you want some oatmeal?

STANLEY. Un-uh.

BERTHA. Well, honey, how 'bout some of those biscuits?

STANLEY. Un-uhhhh.

BERTHA. Will you try some hash browns?

STANLEY. Oh, Mama, get off—I'll get some M & M's on the way to trade school.

BERTHA. Stanley, man cannot live by M & M's alone.

STANLEY. Oh, Mama, get off!

BERTHA. And don't you lie to me about trade school.

Vera Carp said you spent half the morning yesterday sitting in your car out in front of the grocery store.

STANLEY. Well, Vera Carp can kiss my rusty butt.

BERTHA. Stanley, don't you start.

STANLEY. Mama, I'd be just fine if Charlene would stop it.

BERTHA. I wish to God that you and your sister would stop that fighting!

STANLEY. Yeah . . . I heard her up there groanin'.

BERTHA. Stanley, she'll hear you.

STANLEY. Locks the door, turns on the water, starts groanin'.

BERTHA. Stanley!

STANLEY. Every time the groanin' starts, I know she's tryin' to squeeze into another pair of my blue jeans.

BERTHA. Now Stanley, you may be big yourself someday.

STANLEY. If I am—shoot me.

BERTHA. Stanley!

STANLEY. Mama, she ripped out three pair of Wranglers in the last month.

BERTHA. Charlene! Charlene, I know you can hear me. Get out of Stanley's jeans now!

STANLEY. Yeah, her hips are so big she has to lay down on the bed and groan into them.

BERTHA. Stanley, will you stop it! Now we're gonna find her a good diet.

STANLEY. You better find her a good surgeon.

BERTHA. Stanley! Get out of here before you drive me to a rubber room at Big Springs! Charlene! Charlene! You get out of Stanley's jeans. You know you're too big to fit in 'em. It just breaks my heart to hurt that baby's feelings.

STANLEY. (*as he exits*) Yeah . . . I shoulda known you'd take her side. (*STANLEY changes to CHARLENE.*)

BERTHA. Stanley, don't let those dogs in the house! Get out of here! ! . . . Thunder, get off that chair; you know better. You better get out that door. Look at this mess, and I just cleaned this house. Oh, my God, Bingo, what is that? Oh, no! Get out of here! Now wait. Come back here and take that with you! Go on, get out! You dogs are gonna be the death of me . . . Charlene! Charlene, honey, will you hurry up! I know you're working on your poem for the radio show, but sweetheart, your breakfast is getting cold.

CHARLENE. (*offstage*) Mama! Come up here and get this dog out of my room!

BERTHA. Which one?

CHARLENE. (*offstage*) Woffie.

BERTHA. Woffie, come down here. Get on down here. (*whistles*) Come on, Woffie . . . Now listen you — I told you about comin' through that door . . . the next time, I said the next time you come in this house, I know a German Shepherd that's gonna be lookin' for a new home. (*points to another dog*) And you're next! (*CHARLENE enters.*) Charlene, honey, you want some oatmeal?

CHARLENE. No.

BERTHA. Well, how 'bout some biscuits?

CHARLENE. Un-uh.

BERTHA. Will you try some hashbrowns?

CHARLENE. No, thank you.

BERTHA. Well, here honey, at least have a cup of coffee. (*CHARLENE repeatedly scoops sugar into her cup, making sound effects.*) Charlene. Charlene, honey, now stop! Remember that agreement we made that we were gonna use Sweet and Slender in our coffee?

CHARLENE. I used Sweet and Slender when I still had something to live for, Mother.

BERTHA. Oh, honey, what's wrong?

CHARLENE. Nothin'!

BERTHA. Why are you mad?

CHARLENE. I'm not!

BERTHA. Charlene, snap! Now honey, everybody can't be cheerleader.

CHARLENE. Oh, Mother . . .

BERTHA. Well honey, there are other things to live for.

CHARLENE. Name one.

BERTHA. Well, I can't think of any right now, but when I do I'll write 'em down and give 'em to you.

CHARLENE. I'll tell you one thing. If that vicious little Connie Carp calls me "two-bits" one more time, she better send out for bandages.

BERTHA. She's just like her mother. You kill her with kindness.

CHARLENE. I'll kill her with somethin'!

BERTHA. You do unto others . . .

CHARLENE. (*as she exits*) Uh-huh! (*CHARLENE changes to CHAD.*)

BERTHA. And don't let those damn dogs in the house! Get out of here! I wish you would get on that table! Please get on that table! Trixie, Trixie, Dolly, now come on honey, get out. You girls know better. Woffie! You come through that door one more time and you'll need drugs to kill the pain! Now I have had it! (*We hear CHAD HARTFORD offstage, ringing a DOORBELL.*) Oh, it's that reporter. Comin'! (*She checks her appearance. RINNNNNGGG!*) I said I was comin'! (*RINNNNNGGGGGG!*) Well, you'll just have to hold onto your horses! I said I was comin'! (*RINNNGGG.*

RINNNGGGG. RINNNGGGG. CHAD enters.) Yes?

CHAD. Mrs. Bumiller?

BERTHA. Yes.

CHAD. My name is Chad Hartford.

BERTHA. Oh, come in, Mr. Hartford. Could I get you somethin' to drink? A cup of coffee?

CHAD. I don't care for anything to drink. I'm in a bit of a hurry. Could we get right to the interview?

BERTHA. Well, certainly.

CHAD. Now, you are chairing the Censorship of the Text Books Committee, am I correct?

BERTHA. Oh, no no no no. That's the Reverend Spikes who heads that committee . . . although I am a member. We're gonna have a meetin' this afternoon by the way. But please, don't come. The Reverend Spikes, he just hates the press. I think it's because of all those old folks' homes he owns, and all them terrible things they said about him in the newspapers. Well, I better shut up. Anyway, I head the subcommittee that wants to snatch the books off the shelves of the local high school library. Some of those books are absolutely disgusting. Our children have no business reading them, and somebody has got to protect the minds of the children.

CHAD. Before we get to the books, Mrs. Bumiller, could you tell me what in your background do you feel qualifies you to censor library books?

BERTHA. Well, I can briefly list my activities, if you like.

CHAD. Please.

BERTHA. Well, I'm currently president of the Ladies for a Better Tuna. I am den mother for Den 225. I'm the only high-C soprano in the First Baptist Choir. And I'm currently recorder of the Javalina Club; that's a women's auxiliary of the Wild Hogs. It's kind of a break-off of the Lions Club. We just thought the Lions were too liberal. I'm the former head of the local B.B.B., that's the Better Baptist Bureau. And I'm a member of our shut-in visiting squad, the Tuna Helpers. And I'm currently president and co-founder of Citizens for Fewer Blacks in Literature.

CHAD. Thank you, Mrs. Bumiller. I think I get the idea.

BERTHA. Well, all right.

CHAD. Now, exactly what are the books that you think should be removed from the shelves?

BERTHA. Well, now there's four of 'em that we're gonna try and have removed nationwide. And then we're gonna go from there.

CHAD. What are the four books, Mrs. Bumiller?

BERTHA. *Roots.* Now, we don't deny that *Roots* has been a very popular TV series, but we feel it only shows one side of the slavery issue.

CHAD. Go on . . .

BERTHA. *Bury My Heart at Wounded Knee.* Well, it's the most disgusting title to begin with; it just makes me want to erp. It villifies a great American, General Custer. And it encourages the reader to believe that the United States Government can't be trusted in makin' any treaties.

CHAD. What's next?

BERTHA. *Huckleberry Finn,* by Mark Twain.

CHAD. Did he write that?

BERTHA. Uh huh. Now, that book shows a pre-teenage boy avoidin' his chores, runnin' away from home, cohortin' with a Negro convict, and puttin' on women's clothes.

CHAD. Go on . . .

BERTHA. *Romeo and Juliet.*

CHAD. What, pray tell, is wrong with *Romeo and Juliet?*

BERTHA. It just shows sex among teenagers, that's all. And we're not for that, and we're certainly not going to encourage it. Besides, it shows a rampant disrespect for parental authority.

CHAD. You are aware that William Shakespeare wrote that play?

BERTHA. Oh, yes we are. And we're lookin' into the rest of his stuff too. He wrote *Barefoot in the Park,* didn't he?

CHAD. (*pause*) Mrs. Bumiller, quite often these days, people claim to talk to God. Do you talk to God?

BERTHA. Well, I pray.

CHAD. I didn't ask you that, Mrs. Bumiller. I asked if you talk to God directly?

BERTHA. Well no, I don't. But he leaves little messages for me . . . with the Reverend Spikes. And second-hand messages from the Lord is good enough for me.

CHAD. Thank you Mrs. Bumiller. I think we got one hell of a story here.

BERTHA. Don't you rush off. I've got other interesting things to tell you about Tuna.

CHAD. Well, I'm sure it just boggles the mind, Mrs. Bumiller, but I really must run.

BERTHA. Now, wait a minute. What was the name of your magazine?

CHAD. *Intellect.*

BERTHA. I don't believe we have that here in Tuna.

CHAD. I'll see that you get a copy. Goodbye, Mrs. Bumiller. (*CHAD exits and changes to PETEY.*)

BERTHA. Well, bye. Well, I think reporters just ask the silliest questions. Well, I guess I'm lucky he didn't ask more than he did. Thank God he didn't ask me about my family. Poor Charlene. That girl, she's just going crazy over not getting cheerleader. I said, "Charlene, honey, settle down, it'll be fine. You'll get cheerleader next year." And she looks at me with tears streaming down her cheeks and says, "Mama, I'm a senior." I don't know how to tell my only daughter she's never gonna be a cheerleader. I just don't know how to do it. Oooohhh, and Stanley. I swear I don't know what I'm gonna do with that boy, datin' that Mexican girl. He never has been right. Oh, but Jody's going to be O.K., except that he's got eight to ten dogs following him all the time, but he'll grow out of that. I know he will. I hope. (*BERTHA takes out knife and begins to prepare vegetables.*) At least I didn't have to lie about Hank. I swear, I've cooked and cleaned for that sorry son-of-a-bitch . . . for 27 years, and he won't even take me to the drive-in movies. Of course, I pretend not to notice as we go to church on Sunday morning, after Saturday night. After I've smelled the perfume and seen the lipstick smears. I swear, sometimes I just wish that man would have a stroke! I swear I do! . . . I don't mean that . . . God, forgive me. I don't mean that. I am so glad that reporter didn't ask.

(*MUSIC; then BERTHA turns on radio. ON TAPE:*)

ARLES. (*tape*) This is Arles Struvie with the news update, concerning the recently deceased Judge Roscoe Buckner, who died yesterday. Now the body was found by Nickey Mayberry, who'd come over to collect for the newspaper; Nickey wishes to quelch all rumors that the Judge was found dead in a woman's bikini swim suit. He says there's no truth to that rumor whatsoever.

THURSTON (*tape*) It's not true.

Arles (*tape*) It's not.

Thurston (*tape*) It's not.

Arles (*tape*) It's not. It's not. According to Nickey, it was a 1950 turquoise, Dale Evans, one-piece swimming suit, with lots of cow-gal fringe. Services are pending at Hubert Funeral Home.

Thurston (*tape*) Ain't that awful. Ain't that awful.

Arles (*tape*) Gahhh!!!

(*PETEY FISK enters. BERTHA reads the National Enquirer, and becomes YIPPY by covering her face with it.*)

Petey. This is Petey Fisk, speaking to you for the Greater Tuna Humane Society.

Bertha as Yippy. Yip yip

Petey. I'm here to introduce this week's pet-of-the-week.

Yippy. Yip yip yip

Petey. His name is Yippy-yi-yi-yeh.

Yippy. Yip yip

Petey. But we just call him Yippy.

Yippy. Yip yip yip

Petey. That's why.

Yippy. Yip yip yip

Petey. This is Yippy's fifth appearance as pet-of-the-week . . .

Yippy. Yip yip yip

Petey. . . . And this charming little part rat-terrier, part chihuahua will make a lovely pet for someone.

Yippy. Yip

Petey. We're sure.

Yippy. Yip yip yip

PETEY. Stop it! His only real drawback as a pet is a tendency to hyperactive behavior.

YIPPY. Yip yip yip yip yip yip

PETEY. Stop it! As you can understand, we here at the Humane Society quite often have trouble giving away small, shrill animals.

YIPPY. Yip yip yip

PETEY. But we still have hope for Yippy.

YIPPY. Yip yip

PETEY. We know there must be some deaf person out there who would love to have a dog, and who would make the perfect owner for Yippy. Now, if there's any deaf person out there listening who wants this dog, please call me, Petey Fisk, at 477-7777.

YIPPY. Yip yip yip yip

PETEY. Call anytime, day or night.

YIPPY. Yip yip	PETEY. PLEASE call!
YIPPY. Yip yip	PETEY. If you're out of town, call collect.
YIPPY. Yip yip yip	PETEY. I gotta get rid of this dog!

YIPPY. Yip yip

PETEY. This is Petey Fisk, speaking to you for the Greater Tuna Humane Society.

| YIPPY. Yip yip | PETEY. Thank you. |
| YIPPY. Yip yip yip yip | |

(*PETEY exits. BERTHA turns off radio and dials phone, making sound effects. One ring from her point of view, then a loud ring; PETEY enters and answers phone.*)

PETEY. Hello.

BERTHA. Hello, Petey? Is this Petey Fisk?

PETEY. Yes.

BERTHA. This is Bertha Bumiller, Petey, and I wanna talk to you, and I want you to listen. Do you understand, Petey?

PETEY. What're you talkin' . . .

BERTHA. I said I wanna talk and I want you to listen. Petey, I have tried to think what I have done to deserve this life I lead. A husband who spent four years in prison for robbin' a fillin' station of forty-seven dollars. And there are my psycho twins, Charlene and Stanley, who you know have caused me no end of grief. And my youngest, Jody, is never seen that he doesn't have a pack of dogs around him. They follow him to school. They follow him home. They follow him everywhere. And last week, Petey, I nearly had to whup him because he wanted to take 'em to the First Baptist Church!

PETEY. Well, now, Bertha . . .

BERTHA. I said, I talk. And you listen. Now, Petey, we have a very serious situation on our hands. My son Jody has something as bad as a drug habit. Jody has a dog habit. He has a psychological addiction to those dogs, and you, Petey Fisk, you're a puppy pusher!

PETEY. Well, I never . . .

BERTHA. I said I-talk-and-you-listen! Now, I will put up with Shep, Woffie, Trixie, Bingo, Blossom, Sweet Nothin', Dolly and Thunder, but if that little Yippy-half-rat, half-chihuahua, half-whatever that you been talkin' about on the radio . . . if that dog shows up at my house, Petey Fisk, they'll have to drag the river to find your body!

PETEY. But I . . . I . . .

BERTHA. I said listen! Now, Petey, I'm gonna call my Aunt Pearl Burras . . . I swear to God, I'm gonna call my Aunt Pearl, and I'm gonna tell her to make up a whole batch of her bitter pills. I mean business. I'm as serious as a stroke. I will not be the mother of an addict, whether he's on opium or bassett hounds. Now say goodbye Petey. (*BERTHA hangs up and exits, and changes to LEONARD.*)

PETEY. Good-bye. (*He hangs up and exits, and changes to DIDI. On the radio, we hear—ON TAPE:*)

ARLES. (*tape*) We interrupt this program with a news update. The recent sighting of a U.F.O., that is an unidentified flying object, by R.R. Snavely has been discounted by his wife, Didi. According to Didi, R.R. was drunk when he actually claimed to have sighted it. So she says everybody just forget about it, he was drunk.

THURSTON. (*tape*) Well, we all thought it was somethin' like that.

ARLES. (*tape*) We did.

THURSTON. (*tape*) We did.

ARLES. (*tape*) We did.

THURSTON. (*tape*) We did. Hell, it had to be.

ARLES. (*tape*) And now folks, sit back and listen to the number one show in Dewey County. On The Line With Leonard. Where your business is everybody's business. And now here's station manager Leonard Childers.

(*MUSIC. LEONARD enters.*)

LEONARD. Hello everybody! This is Leonard Childers. Coming into your homes through Radio Station OKKK. Where every day we take a few minutes to find out just what's up Tuna's craw . . . Now I see the lines're already lighting up and we'll be takin' our first let-it-out call after we take a quick look at "This Week

in Tuna." I got a message here from the Reverend
Spikes over at the Coweta Baptist Church; he says he's
gonna sponsor another record-burning. He says to bring
all your rock-and-roll, and this time be sure and get
your Chuck Berry and your Brenda Lee and your Little
Richard. He says, leave that Buddy Holly and Elvis at
home; they're good Southern boys and they'll be
forgiven. Anyway, that'll be this comin' Sunday night at
eight o'clock down at the Coweta Baptist Church. So
bring your rock-and-roll, come on out and burn it . . .
Let's see what else we have here . . . Ida Thompson has
organized another trip up to the Eureka Springs Passion
Play over in Arkansas. Ida says if you've signed up,
they're going to be leaving this Saturday morning at 7:45
a.m. from the First Methodist parking lot, and Ida says
if you're not there by 7:45, she's goin' to leave ya . . . All
right folks, let's get to our first caller. (*He punches the
imaginary line.*) You're on the line with Leonard. Let it
out! (*DIDI enters.*)

DIDI. Leonard, Didi Snavely. (*AMPLIFIED FEED-
BACK*)

LEONARD. Didi! Turn that radio down! Folks, you
have to remember to turn your radio down when you
call in 'cause it just blows the hell out of my ears! Let it
out, Didi.

DIDI. Leonard? Can't something be done about those
Halloween pranksters?

LEONARD. Kinda early for Halloween, ain't it Didi?

DIDI. Leonard, you wouldn't feel that way if you
knew what I'd been through. Now, Leonard, soapin'
windows and lettin' the air out of tires is one thing. But I
draw the line at extreme mental anguish. Do you hear
me, Leonard?

LEONARD. I hear you, Didi.

DIDI. Last year, those kids came over in the middle of the night and poured sorghum syrup all over my front porch.

LEONARD. That's real mean.

DIDI. Oh, I'm just gettin' started. Now, Mama comes over every morning about 5:30 after she's had her prunes. And when poor Mama hit that thick syrup, it stopped her dead in her tracks.

LEONARD. (*laughs*) Oh Didi. That's real mean!

DIDI. It's not funny, Leonard! She was out there for two and a half hours. She watched the sun come up.

LEONARD. Now who could think of anything that mean?

DIDI. I'm sure that Virgil Carp was in on it. But I can't prove nothing.

LEONARD. Sounds like something Virgil would do.

DIDI. Well, if I catch him near my house, he better have a high threshold to pain.

LEONARD. Now Didi, we all know you wouldn't hurt that boy . . .

DIDI. Hide and watch, Leonard. Hide and watch.

LEONARD. Virgil, I'll tell you son, if you're listening, the woman means business.

DIDI. But Leonard, the damage is already done. I can't even pour syrup over my pancakes without thinking of that poor little old lady trying to reach that doorbell.

LEONARD. Just settle down, Didi; ain't no use gettin' upset. Take one of your nerve pills.

DIDI. I believe I will. (*She hangs up and exits, and changes to PHINAS.*)

LEONARD. (*clicks her off*) Thank you Didi. Folks, it's gettin' so the kids can't have any fun anymore. But you know, Didi has a rough life down there running that

store. She's got a lot to let out . . . (*PHINAS enters;*
LEONARD punches the line.) Hello! You're on the line
with Leonard. Let it out . . . (*pause*) Hello, you're on
the line.

PHINAS. Am I on? (*FEEDBACK*)

LEONARD. Turn it down!

PHINAS. Sorry, I forgot!

LEONARD. God!

PHINAS. This is Phinas Blye.

LEONARD. What's up, Phinas?

PHINAS. I'm calling to announce I will be a candidate
for Tuna's City Council in next year's elections.

LEONARD. Now Phinas, you've been running for City
Council for as long as I can remember. Why don't you
just give up?

PHINAS. Well, you know, it's funny. Ha haaa
(*laughs*). Now, in the past elections, my opponents have
made personality a major issue. Let's face it, in a personality contest, I'm always going to lose. I mean, I'm
short, and I was born in Indiana, and a lot of people
just naturally seem to hate me.

LEONARD. You're right there, Phinas.

PHINAS. But this year, I'm injecting new and vital
issues that cannot be ignored by the voters. Did you
know, for example, that there're thousands of citizens in
this country who pay no taxes whatsoever.

LEONARD. Like who, Phinas?

PHINAS. Like welfare mothers and prisoners!

LEONARD. They don't pay any?

PHINAS. No! And it would be easy to tax the
prisoners, 'cause everyone knows where they are.

LEONARD. Well, you got a point there, Phinas. And
we wish you the best of luck this time around.

PHINAS. Well, you only have to win once. Ha haaaaa
. . . (*PHINAS hangs up and exits, and changes to STANLEY.*)

LEONARD. (*clicks him off*) Thank you Phinas. I'll tell you, you're a man-ahead-of-his-time. Remember you heard it here first. You know, Phinas has run for City Council now on to fourteen years, and he's never even made it to first base. Hang in there, Phinas. (*punches the line*) Hello, you're on the line with Leonard. Let it out. (*STANLEY enters.*)

STANLEY. Uh, this is Stanley Bumiller.

LEONARD. Now what do you want Stanley? Keep it clean.

STANLEY. I was just listening to your last phone call. And it seems to me if the government is lookin' to tax something, then why don't they put a tax on stupidity?

LEONARD. Now Stanley, this is a serious program. Get to it.

STANLEY. I am serious. I guarantee you one thing, if this country had a stupid tax, Phinas Blye would be in the top bracket.

LEONARD. Stanley, Phinas Blye is a model citizen. Unlike some people I know.

STANLEY. He's an ignorant little idget.

LEONARD. Now Stanley, we don't need to get into any name-calling.

STANLEY. He's a pinhead idiot.

LEONARD. Stanley . . .

STANLEY. Hey Leonard, why don't you tell Phinas Blye to kiss my referendum! (*STANLEY hangs up and exits, and changes to DIDI.*)

LEONARD. (*punches him off*) Now Stanley, you can't say that on the radio! . . . I hate to say anything bad about Hank Bumiller's boy, but we all hoped that year in reform school would have done Stanley some good. But he came out meaner than Mussolini. You just can't help some people, I reckon. All right folks, we have time for one more call. (*punches the line*) Hello, you're on the line with Leonard. Let it out. (*DIDI enters.*)

DIDI. Leonard? Didi Snavely again.

LEONARD. What's the matter this time, Didi?

DIDI. Leonard, can't something be done about those hobos under the interstate bridge?

LEONARD. Out there under that underpass?

DIDI. Oh, Leonard, it's gotten so crowded you can't even dump your garbage there anymore. And stink! You can smell 'em in Coweta County. Now Leonard, there is enough soap in the world to keep everybody clean. Am I wrong?

LEONARD. I believe you're right, Didi.

DIDI. And instead of minding the store, my husband R.R. goes down there and drinks with them.

LEONARD. Now Didi, is that where R.R. spotted that unidentified flying Mexican food?

DIDI. No it isn't. And it's real white of you to bring it up, Leonard. (*MAJOR FEEDBACK as she turns up the radio and puts phone up to the radio speaker.*)

LEONARD. God almighty!

(*DIDI hangs up and exits, and changes to PETEY.
    LEONARD exits and changes to PEARL. MUSIC.
    Then, ON TAPE:*)

ARLES. (*tape*) You've been listening to Leonard on the Line, and this is Arles Struvie. Got a news flash here. Sheriff Givins says Danny Palvadore is out of the state penitentiary and he's headin' home in a 1962 blue Impala. So everybody watch out for 'im; he'll run over you.

THURSTON. (*tape*) He will.

ARLES. (*tape*) He will. He will. Hell, the man will kill you.

THURSTON. (*tape*) Ohhh! And now for that weather report, we're going to go out there to Buckner Basin with Harold Dean Lattimer. Harold Dean, what's it gonna be?

HAROLD DEAN. (*tape*) Well, in the weather, it's gonna rain . . .

(*PETEY enters and turns off radio, and begins to write letter.*)

PETEY. Mrs. Pearl Burras, General Delivery, Tuna, Texas. (*PEARL enters.*) Dear Mrs. Burras. After a recent unsettling phone call from your niece Bertha Bumiller, I feel compelled to write to you. As you know, relations have never been strong between the Humane Society and those who raise chickens. We do understand that this is your livelihood, disgusting as it may be to those of us here at the Humane Society.

PEARL. (*feeding chickens*) Here chick, chick, chick, chickie. Come and get it babies. Eat it up, eat it up. Babies, babies, babies . . .

PETEY. We do feel, however, that you are posing a danger to the children of your neighborhood, as well as their pets. We're sure you love the kids of your neighborhood as much as we do.

PEARL. (*spotting children in her yard*) Get out of those tomatoes! Get out of 'em! I'm gonna call Sheriff Givens . . . Let me at 'em.

PETEY. Mrs. Burras, we have traced over seventy dog-poisonings to your doorstep. Now, don't you think you've taken eccentricity a bit too far?

PEARL. Oh, they've left that poodle in my yard. I'll bet it's an egg-sucker! Where is it?

PETEY. We feel that you have been somewhat over-zealous in the protection of your chickens.

PEARL. Where's my strychnine? Please to God, don't tell me I'm out!

PETEY. In fact, Mrs. Burras, there are those of us at the Humane Society who believe that you actually enjoy poisoning dogs.

PEARL. I'll kill Henry if he's hidden my strychnine!

PETEY. We are well aware of your "bitter pills", those strychnine-laced biscuits rolled into enticing little dough balls.

PEARL. Oh, I found it. Henry thought he'd be smart and hide it, but I found it. I'm gonna kill me a poodle. Now, where's my biscuits? I'm gonna make you a bitter pill.

PETEY. We are also aware that your husband Henry is the owner of Ripper, the finest bird dog in Dewey County. How could anybody who lives around a $2,000 dog like Ripper poison people's puppies so heartlessly?

PEARL. Here puppy, puppy, puppy. Get over here, egglips. Come here and get the bitter pill . . . Get back, Ripper! It's not for you. You stay back! Get back; it's not for you, Ripper. . . . Oh, I didn't mean to scare you; now come on. I'll set it down right here—and you come and get it . . . Ripper! Don't eat that! Oh my God, Ripper's eaten the bitter pill!

PETEY. Mrs. Burras, you have classic symptoms of canicidal thumbitus, a psychological disorder that causes you to want to kill other people's dogs, for real or imagined reasons.

PEARL. Oh my God, I've poisoned Henry's bird dog . . . Oh, look at him shake.

PETEY. Now the only known cure for canicidal thumbitus is to surround the patient with lots and lots of dogs until the urge to kill passes.

PEARL. Oh, what am I going to do? Oh, think Pearl, think. Think think think. Oh, I know what I'll do. I know what I'll do! I'll call Stanley; I'll have him come over here and drag that dog out in the road. We'll run over it with the Pontiac. We'll tell Henry it got hit by a car.

PETEY. And are you in luck, Mrs. Burras. The Humane Society has a one-way bus ticket for you to Dallas, to the Texas State Dog Fair, where you can be surrounded by over four thousand dogs.

PEARL. (*dialing phone*) That's what I'll do. I'll call Stanley. I can count on Stanley.

PETEY. Mrs. Burras—if you make it through the entire show without poisoning a single animal, the Humane Society will pay your bus fare home. Think, you can find peace of mind, and the dogs of your neighborhood can have a respite from the death and carnage to which they have been subjected. Sincerely, Petey Fisk, Greater Tuna Humane Society. (*PETEY exits and changes to STANLEY.*)

PEARL. Hello Stanley, this is Pearl. Get over here quick, I need you . . . I want you to run over Henry's bird dog . . . Ripper . . . Umhmm . . . Well, he's already dead . . . I killed him . . . Oh, Stanley, I know it's not as much fun running over a dead dog! But please to God, get over here. I don't believe I can stand it . . .

You're a good nephew . . . I'll see you in a minute . . .
All right. Goodbye. (*She hangs up.*) Oh, I knew I could
count on Stanley. Oh, and while he's here, I'll get him to
run me down to the funeral parlor so I can view Judge
Buckner. Oh Lord, nothing would get me out in this
heat except to see him dead. I just want to see for
myself. Make for sure.

STANLEY. (*offstage*) Pearl!

PEARL. Stanley, is that you? Come in, come in.
(*STANLEY enters.*)

STANLEY. Pearl, how come you poisoned Uncle
Henry's bird dog?

PEARL. Oh, don't say that, Stanley. I didn't. It was an
accident. I was after an egg-suckin' poodle, and Ripper
just came up and snatched the bitter pill.

STANLEY. Why hell, Pearl, I always kinda liked ol'
Ripper.

PEARL. Well . . .

STANLEY. You know, when Uncle Henry finds out
you poisoned a $2,000 dog, he's gonna have a kiniption
fit.

PEARL. Oh, Stanley, he'll scream like a banshee . . .
Quick, drag that dog out in the road. We'll run over it.

STANLEY. Hell Pearl, you're crazy.

PEARL. Oh Stanley, don't you say that. I'm not . . .
Oh, and Stanley, I want you to take me down to the
funeral parlor so I can view Judge Buckner. You can
wait for me at the Tasty Freeze. I'll buy you an ice cream
cone.

STANLEY. All right, hurry up, Pearl, get in the car.

PEARL. I'm comin'.

STANLEY. Oh, come on, Pearl, hurry up. I don't want
nobody to see this.

PEARL. Don't rush me, Stanley. I'm an old woman.

(*They get in the car. STANLEY reaches to turn the ignition and we hear the sound of a car trying to start.*) Pump it. (*The car starts.*) Now Stanley, you make it look good.

STANLEY. All right. (*They pull off. There is a definite bump as they run over Ripper.*)

PEARL. Ohhh . . .

(*MUSIC.*)

END OF ACT I

ACT TWO

MUSIC: as intermission ends. BLACKOUT, then LIGHTS up on the parlor at Hubert's Funeral Home. MUSIC: "In the Sweet By-and-By"

PEARL. Owww, Roscoe, is that you? What have they done to you? My goodness, you look so waxy. Oh, they've waxed you down, Judge, so you'll look good . . . you old son-of-a-bitch. A stroke! It was your conscience that killed you. Those same tight little lips. Well, those beady little eyes will never see the light again, will they, Judge? Oh, what could have ever made me want to love you? Tell me, how-how-how-how could I? I guess a young girl can be foolish. But then you were always too good for me, now weren't you, Judge? Just too good. That's all right. I took it. But then you sent my favorite nephew Stanley to reform school. And for what? Spray-painting stop signs! Oh, Judge, you might as well have killed him. He's never been the same. I told you then I'd sing over your grave when you died . . . And Judge, I feel a song comin' on! (*She sings.*) "Oh, the fox went out one stormy night. He prayed for the moon to give him light. He said 'I got many a mile to go, before I reach the town-o, town-o, town-ooooooo . . .'"

(*VERA CARP enters.*)

VERA. Why Pearl Burras, is that you?
PEARL. Vera Carp, how are you?
VERA. (*speaks to non-appearing son*) Virgil, honey,

38

wait out there in the lobby. Be reverent. (*to PEARL*)
Ohhh, I haven't seen you in so long.

PEARL. It's been a long time, Vera.

VERA. (*referring to Judge*) Ain't it awful?

PEARL. Doesn't he look lovely?

VERA. I suppose. (*to Virgil*) Virgil, I mean it.

PEARL. I think he makes a lovely lookin' corpse.
Don't you think he looks nice?

VERA. Well, no, I don't. (*to Virgil*) Virgil, that's to
sign your name in, not to draw in. Quit it now! (*to
PEARL*) Well, Pearl, I just don't know what to say . . .
one dead body just looks like another dead body to me.
They just look dead and still and . . .

VERA & PEARL. . . . waxy.

VERA. (*to Virgil*) Virgil, I'm gonna knock you into
next week if you pick another flower! Go on. Go. Wait
in the station wagon with Connie!

PEARL. Vera, that boy's not right.

VERA. Glass houses . . . Well, Pearl, Judge Buckner
has met his maker at last. (*VERA exits and changes to
STANLEY.*)

PEARL. In a Dale Evans swimsuit. Oh, Judge, I don't
believe I can stand it! (*SHE sings as she exits.*) "Oh the
fox went out one stormy night. He prayed for the moon
to give him light. He said 'I got many a mile to
go, before I reach the town-o, town-o, town-
ooooooo. . .'"

(*MUSIC: "An old-fashioned spiritual hymn" as
    PEARL exits and changes to THURSTON.
    STANLEY enters.*)

STANLEY. Guess who! Well, don't you look just like
yourself? Don't you though, your honor? Dead. You
can't imagine how safe I feel. 'Course, I had a lotta time

to think about it while I was in reform school. That's about all I can say for Gatesville. Plenty of time to think. Yeah, Judge, I had to nuzzle up to that homely housekeeper of yours. Yolanda. She thought I was in love. Oh, I kept it up 'til I got me a copy of all her keys. And I got all my information bit by bit. Ya know, like her schedule and your schedule and that one hour — that one hour on Wednesday morning when you were all alone. When she went out to buy groceries. Yeah, I found out about that, and I set you up. I just parked across from the Piggly Wiggly and waited. And when I seen Yolanda go into that store, I done a beeline to your house. Drove right up the curvin' driveway. Walked right through the goddamned front door, right up the stairs to your bedroom. And all you could do was lay there on your half-paralyzed ass and stare, but you knew what I was there for, didn't you? You knew! Man, it was hell gettin' you into that swimsuit! It was worth it. But you wanna know what my favorite part was? Huh? You wanna know what my favorite part was, your honor? It was when I pulled out that syringe, and you started pleading with me. You pleading with me! And all it took to finish you off was a few air bubbles, right in the vein . . . just a few little air bubbles — stroke! I guess we're even. Then why don't I feel like it, huh? You know, someday, after my mama's dead, I may just turn myself in. Won't everybody be surprised? Oh, I can hear 'em now: "Why, who would have thought Stanley Bumiller would have the brains to pull that off?" Sheee . . .

(*MUSIC: "the same old-fashioned spiritual hymn" as STANLEY exits and changes to CHARLENE. THURSTON enters.*)

THURSTON. Good afternoon, Tuna. This is Thurston Wheelis, and this is the Wheelis-Struvie Midday Report. First off in the news, there's gonna be a meeting of the Smut Snatchers of the New Order this afternoon at the Coweta Baptist Church, startin' about five o'clock. Now, Radio Station OKKK is gonna carry that meetin' live. So you tune in. Now, the Smut Snatchers' latest project is cleaning up those dictionaries down at Tuna High School. And they say, if you know of a word that you feel has questionable value, or a word that you feel just should not be in the dictionary — now if you don't want your child around the word, bring that word with you to the meeting. Bring it to the meeting. The Reverend Spikes says he'll consider each word on a word-by-word basis . . . And now we have a special guest with us today here at Station OKKK. She's a senior at Tuna High School, and the daughter of Hank and Bertha Bumiller — Miss Charlene Bumiller. Now, Charlene is the winner of this year's annual Javalina Club's poetry writing contest, and if she wins next month in Wichita Falls, she's goin' on to the national competition held up in Butte, Montana, come February . . . why in the hell they'd wanna have it there, I'll never know. But anyway, Charlene says her poem registers her love and admiration for Tuna. Here's Charlene now, and her poem speaks for itself. (*CHARLENE enters.*)

CHARLENE. "My Tuna" by Charlene Bumiller.
My Tuna, oh my Tuna
The only place I know
I've often thought of leaving you
But don't know where I'd go.

For Paris has no bar-b-que

And Rome just can't compare
To a lovely Texas sunset
When the dust is in the air.

Tuna, oh my Tuna,
Is such fun on Friday nights
When the Jaguars lose another game
And everybody fights.

And I love you when you're frozen
And I love you when you're dry
And in April when the pollen
Is so thick it makes you cry.

But Tuna, oh my Tuna,
Please stay just the way you are
'Cause I just think the world
Outside of Tuna is bizarre.

(CHARLENE exits and changes to ARLES.)

THURSTON. That's real good, sweetheart. Doesn't that just warm the cockles of your heart? Thank you, Charlene! . . . Got a call today from Nadine Wooton's mother, Norma. She says Nadine is standing out along the highway again with her suitcase. Now, as most of you folks know, about this time every year, poor Nadine stands out along Route 4 with her suitcase. Now don't try and pick her up, 'cause she'll only tell you she's waitin' on Mr. Monahue. So we just thought we'd remind you to look out for her; don't run her over, and don't try to pick her up. *(ARLES enters.)* Well, it looks like it's that time of the year.

ARLES. It is.

THURSTON. It is.

ARLES. It is. It is. It is. Well folks, next up in the news. Juanelle Rainey is not dead.

THURSTON. No, she's not.

ARLES. She's not. She's not. Now as you all know, Juanelle's been in the hospital for about eight months with a combination of fatal diseases; I don't know, how many did she have?

THURSTON. Well, I don't remember, Arles, but it was awful.

ARLES. It was awful. I thought she was gonna die. She thought she was gonna die. We all thought she was gonna die.

THURSTON. We did.

ARLES. We did. We did. But she didn't.

THURSTON. No, she didn't.

ARLES. She didn't. And she's home and she says everybody drop by and see her, give her a ring—she's not dead.

THURSTON. She's okay.

ARLES. She is. She is. She is.

THURSTON. She is.

ARLES. Now folks, it's time for a little culture. (*THURSTON exits and changes to R.R.*) In keeping with the government's new policy of allowing private enterprise to contribute to America's artistic needs, Radio Station OKKK is proud to present the weekly art minute. And this week's guest is none other than Tuna's own R.R. Snavely. What've you got for us today, R.R.? (*R.R. SNAVELY enters.*)

R.R. "Honky Tonk Angels."

ARLES. "Honky Tonk Angels." Take it away, R.R.

R.R. Well, I gotta warm up first, Arles. (*He warms up on his imaginary violin, making sound effects.*)

ARLES. Well now hurry up R.R., you've only got forty seconds left. (*R.R. plays violin for about fifteen seconds.*) Thank you, R.R. Your minute is up. (*R.R. exits and changes back to THURSTON.*) Wasn't that somethin'? Wasn't that somethin'? I tell ya, for an old coot who sees unidentified flying chalupas, he plays a mean fiddle. (*THURSTON enters.*)

THURSTON. He does.

ARLES. He does. He does . . . Now next up in the news, Maxie Bovine, the reigning Miss Tuna in the Miss Texas pageant, has had a run of real bad luck. It seems her talent competition went over by twenty seconds. As you know, Maxie does the famous Scarlett O'Hara I'll-never-eat-a-root-again scene. And just as she got the root to her lips, the buzzer went off. They say Maxie threw a wall-eyed fit, and is still in the hospital suffering from shock, but we talked to her chaperone, Mildred Jean Perkins, and she said Maxie'll be there for that swimsuit competition tomorrow night. That gal's a trouper.

THURSTON. She is.

ARLES. She is.

THURSTON & ARLES. She is. She is.

ARLES. And from our National News Desk: Nuclear accident imperils millions in seven states—Texas not in-cluded.

THURSTON. Um-hmmm.

ARLES. Well, that's all the news we got for ya, but don't touch that dial . . .

THURSTON. Don't touch that dial . . . Get away from it!

ARLES. Get away from it! 'Cause Tuna Speaks is next.

(*MUSIC. THURSTON & ARLES exit. THURSTON*

changes to ELMER, ARLES changes to PETEY. PETEY enters.)

PETEY. This is Petey Fisk, speaking to you for the Greater Tuna Humane Society. You know, we receive a whole lot of flak here at the Humane Society, saying we're insensitive to the needs of fish. Now this is not true. We care a great deal about fish. We understand that when you take a fish out of the water with a hook in its mouth, r-r-rip it through its jaw, and take out a knife and stick it in its anal opening and cut up to its neck, and scrape its insides out, that fish feels that. Fish feel pain. They're just very very subtle about expressing it. So please join the growing number of Americans who prefer their fish in rivers and streams and not on a plate with tater tots. This is Petey Fisk for the Greater Tuna Humane Society. Thank you. (*PETEY exits and changes to VERA. ELMER enters.*)

ELMER. This is Elmer Watkins on Tuna Speaks. As a citizen of Tuna, I feel it's my obligation to speak up about this Agent Orange stuff and its effects on servicemen. I just wanna say that in the last year I've hired fourteen veterans, Viet Nam veterans, to work for me on my road crew, and out of those fourteen, only four of 'em have died, but there wasn't a one of 'em turned orange. I swear to God, not a one of 'em turned anyways near orange. I think it's just more of this propaganda by this liberal press and these hippie-oriented groups. So I think it's time somebody spoke up about this Agent Orange stuff. This is Elmer Watkins on Tuna Speaks. Thank you.

(*ELMER exits and changes to the REVEREND SPIKES. MUSIC: "When the Roll is Called Up Yonder". VERA enters.*)

VERA. (*to an audience member*) Oh—Hiii. Vera
Carp. Welcome to Coweta Baptist Church, where
everybody's welcome. Even Catholics. (*to another*) Hi.
How are you? Isn't that just the prettiest dress. I used to
have one just like that—years ago . . . Isn't it wonderful
how some people can just wear anything! (*to another*)
Why, I thought you were dead! I don't remember who
told me that, but I'm so glad they were wrong. (*to
another*) How are you? (*to another*) How're you?
(*VERA begins meeting.*) I, Vera Carp, Vice-President
of the Smut Snatchers of the New Order, in the absence
of our president, the Reverend Spikes, do hereby
declare this meeting to be officially open. (*She bangs
imaginary gavel.*) Now, we need to send out a communique from our education committee. Now after all the
vicious things they've said about us in the newspapers,
we've decided to become more flexible on bi-lingual
education, and we do indeed have a bi-lingual education
program to submit to the Tuna schools. The difference
is, our program is one of moderation. It entails learning
the following Spanish phrases.

(*The following are pronounced with a distinct East
Texas accent:*)

"Habla, usted ingles?", which means, "Do you speak
English?"; "Cuanto?", which means, "How much?";
"Donde puedo cambiar este cheque?", which is "Where
can I cash this traveller's check?"; "Por favor, envieme
un botones para recoger mi equipaje", which is "Please
send me a boy for my luggage"; and the last one is "No
he pedido esto", which is "I didn't order this!" Now
that's all the Spanish any red-blooded American oughta
feel obligated to learn. Now let's just see the newspapers

make fun of that! . . . Well, he's still not here, so I'm gonna forge ahead. We need to send out a snatch squad . . . Well, we do. We need to send out a book-snatchin' squad to the Tuna High School Library to check those dictionaries. Now, we have a new list of words that have been declared possibly offensive or misunderstandable to pre-college students. Now the words are: hot, hooker, coke, clap, deflower, ball, knocker and nuts. Now after much prayer and soulsearching with the Lord, the Committee has decided not to include the word snatch on this year's list. We know some of you have very strong feelings about snatch, but we just can't afford to change our letterhead at this time. (*SPIKES enters.*) Well, here he is. I hereby turn this meetin' over to our honorable president, the Reverend Spikes. (*She bangs imaginary gavel again.*)

SPIKES. Thank you Vera. And folks, I'm so sorry I'm so late. But let's get down to business . . . Now, we're gonna send out a book-snatching squad to the Tuna High School library . . .

VERA. (*interrupts*) Oh-oh-oh, I already told 'em that.

SPIKES. Well, Vera, that's all the fun of being president is sending out the snatch artists.

VERA. I'm sorry. I won't do it again.

SPIKES. Please don't . . . All right folks, we got a new communique on our bi-lingual education pro- . . .

VERA. (*interrupts*) Oh-oh-oh, I already told 'em that too.

SPIKES. Well, you just told 'em everything, didn't you?

VERA. Well, what did you expect me to do for fifteen minutes while you weren't here, sing show tunes?

SPIKES. Now Vera, now I'm not gonna get into this power struggle thing right here in front of all these people . . .

VERA. (*interrupts*) Hush . . . hush . . . The radio people are here.

SPIKES. Well so they are. Hello Arles, how are you? . . . Fine, fine . . . how's that? (*to VERA*) Are we ready with the Buckner eulogy?

VERA. Of course.

SPIKES. Yes, we're ready with the Judge Buckner Eulogy. I'll tell you what, Arles, just set 'er up right back there. And when you're ready, just kinda wave your hand . . . Oh — you're ready? All right . . . No, I'm ready . . . Okay . . . Are we live? . . . This is the Reverend Spikes, and I just wanna say — I say I just wanna say a few words, a few words about a friend of mine and a friend of Tuna's. Roscoe Buckner spent his whole life in service to his community, his country and his Lord. (*VERA yawns.*) And we're sure that when the roll is called up yonder, he'll be there. He was a judge who made hay while the sun shined, (*VERA yawns again.*) but always, I say always let a smile be his umbrella. He always kept his sunny side up and always saw the silver lining behind every cloud. A judge who took no wooden nickels nor threw caution to the wind, but looked before he leapt and never got in over his head. No, he kept his head, when all about him were losin' theirs and blaming it on him. He kept a stiff upper lip and his nose to the wheel. (*VERA begins to fall asleep.*) About this man we can truly say, he was one of a kind, a jolly good fellow, which nobody can deny. He was one for all and all for one, and to his own self true. And I can tell you this, he did it his way. He was a serious-minded judge, who let bygones be bygones, but remembered the Alamo. About this man we can truly say, he was the cream in Tuna's coffee. He fought fire with fire, and he kept the home fires burning. And when he couldn't stand the heat, he got out of the kitchen. He would walk that extra mile, he would walk it SOFTLY (*VERA wakes up.*) and he'd carry a big stick. He was a Pepper, a man's man, early to bed, early to rise. He laid his cards on the table, gathered at the river and brought in the sheaves. Hunger was his best pickle . . .

VERA. What the devil does that mean . . .

SPIKES. Hush, Vera. He was a judge who wouldn't fire until he saw the whites of their eyes, but whistled a happy little tune, praised God, and passed that ammunition. For he had not yet begun to fight. For never ever ever did I ever hear the man say die . . . he just did. He was a fine upstanding civil servant, who practiced what he preached, put his best foot forward and his money where his mouth was. And when the going got tough, he was gone . . . It's not easy to find the words to describe such a man. But I've done my best. We commend his soul to you, Lord. I, the Reverend Spikes, recommend him. Amen, Lord. Amen. . . . What's that, Arles? Ohh, noooo . . . Okay . . . This is the Reverend Spikes, and I just wanna say, I just wanna say a few words, a few words about a friend of mine and a friend of Tuna's . . .

(*VERA curls up and falls asleep. Both exit; VERA changes to STANLEY and SPIKES changes to SHERIFF. MUSIC. ON TAPE:*)

THURSTON. (*tape*) This is Thurston Wheelis with a sports flash. This just in. The Tuna High School Jaguars lost their season opener against the Kuhlburg Comanchees. It was a hard-fought contest, but in the end, the purple and green Cats were on the short end of a 48 to nothin' score. Coach Raymond Chassie evaluated the loss this way.

COACH. (*tape*) Well, we lost mainly because we couldn't score. But the fact that they made seven touchdowns was a major factor in the loss also. I don't know which was a bigger factor, but you take away them two things, and it would have been a tie. So I'm real proud of our boys anyway.

ARLES. (*tape*) This is Arles Struvie with the Crime Report. Now according to statistics, crime is down in the Greater Tuna area from this time last year. Now this time last year, there were six arrests, and this year so far we only had four. Sheriff Givens says, though the numbers may still seem high, there's no reason for alarm over Tuna's high crime rate. He says it's mostly the same people getting arrested over and over and over again. Here we have Sheriff Givens himself in an interview taped early this morning.

SHERIFF. (*tape*) Yeah, well, I don't run no country club, that's for sure. Where I come from, jail's supposed to be a, you know, unpleasant experience. And I think it still should be. I really do. And I'll tell you one thing, you can call me old-fashion', but a couple of hundred years ago, law enforcement was a much more rewarding profession than it is today.

(*During the above, STANLEY and SHERIFF enter.*)

ARLES. (*tape*) The sheriff's remarks were recorded early this morning at the Dewey County Jail . . . (*SHERIFF turns off radio.*)

SHERIFF. Here we go again, boy. Seems like some people just can't keep out of trouble. Now can they?

STANLEY. I don't know what you're talkin' about.

SHERIFF. You wouldn't put me on, now, would you,

Stanley? You wouldn't do that to me, would you, boy?
Would you?

STANLEY. (*interrupts*) I don't know what you . . .

SHERIFF. Owwhh, I got evidence. Proof. I got
everything I need to know about you, boy. Some people
are just destined for a life in crime. You know how
much money the state's spent on you — to rehabilitate
you? And just look at you. You're what we call a
habitual.

STANLEY. Hey, hey, hey. You gonna charge me with
anything?

SHERIFF. Yeah, I'm gonna charge your ass, boy. But
first, I'm gonna talk to you about this. (*HE pulls out an
imaginary hypodermic needle.*) Stanley, what are you
doin' with a hypodermic needle in your car? You doin'
drugs, boy?

STANLEY. Hey, you come over here! Come over here
and look at my arms! Well come on. Look at 'em! You
look as close as you want to. You put a magnifying glass
up to my arms. Ain't no needles in my arms.

SHERIFF. I wanna know what you're doin' with a needle in your car, Stanley.

STANLEY. 'Cause my mama's got diabetes, and I carry
an extra needle around in case she has a fit. But there
ain't been nuthin' in that needle but air, Sheriff — nuthin'
but air. Anything wrong with having a hypodermic needle full of air, Sheriff? Is that against the law?

SHERIFF. You think you're real smart, don't you
Stanley? You think you're real smart . . . Well, I got a
witness. That's right, Bumiller, I got a witness. No,
you're not too smart. No, I wouldn't say so, not so
smart; you know, your kind never is. Not too smart.

STANLEY. Hey, you gonna charge me with anything?

SHERIFF. Yeah, I'm gonna charge your ass. You may think we're just a bunch of stupid ol' country boys, but we been keepin' an eye on you.

STANLEY. You gonna charge me, you do it!

SHERIFF. (*pulls gun on Stanley*) Yeah, I'm gonna do it. I'm gonna do it right now.

STANLEY. God damn it!

SHERIFF. (*laughs, puts gun away, and produces two imaginary tickets*) There you go, Stanley—traffic tickets, two of 'em. One for speedin', forty in a twenty zone, and another for no turn signal. Now, the next time you take Yolanda out joy-riding, you just better watch yourself. And you're gonna stay right where you are 'til I get forty-one dollars and twenty-seven cents. Now just how smart do you think you are now, Bumiller? (*STANLEY laughs.*) Damn fool. Good night, boy. Oh, and uh, Stanley, if that phone rings, don't you bother. (*STANLEY laughs and exits, and changes to JODY. SHERIFF changes to AUNT PEARL onstage.*)

PEARL. Oh, dear God, I know that I've done some things in my life I shouldn't have done. And I know you've forgiven me time and time again. But just this once, I ask you, please to God, don't ever let Henry find out about that bird dog. Amen. (*PEARL picks up imaginary phone and dials. We hear the rings from her perspective.*) Oh, Stanley, answer the phone. I know you're home. I'm all out of strychnine, and I know you've got some. Well, I guess I'll just have to wait 'til tomorrow. But I don't sleep as well knowing there's no strychnine in the house. (*Phone rings loudly. PEARL hangs up and exits, and changes to HANK. JODY runs in to answer the phone—too late.*)

JODY. Hello? Hello?

(*Hangs up. Turns on radio. MUSIC. ON TAPE:*)

LEONARD. (*tape*) This is Leonard Childers with the Tuna Bulletin Board. Now, if you have any younguns between the ages of eight and fourteen, you need to know that Thursday is your last day to register your kids for Colonel Sprayberry's Character Camp and Survival Institute. Now this year, they're offering classes in Old Testament appreciation, segregation in the Scriptures, Christian biology, character development, and the proper use of firearms. So register your kids today; it will do them some good.

(*MUSIC fades in. HANK enters, turns off radio.*)

HANK. Jody, you listen to that thing too much, son. I want you to leave it off . . . Now, I'm goin' out to check on them hired hands, make sure they ain't out gettin' drunk when they oughta be restin' for the job. I'll be comin' in late. You tell your Mama.

JODY. Why don't you tell Mama?

HANK. 'Cause I told you to! And I want this damn thing off! (*HANK starts to exit.*)

HANK as BERTHA. Hank? (*HANK exits and changes to BERTHA.*)

JODY. He's gone, Mama.

BERTHA. (*offstage*) Gone, honey? Gone where?

JODY. Well, he went out to check on them hired hands, make sure they ain't out gettin' drunk . . .

BERTHA. (*offstage; pause*) Well, Jody, come on up to bed now, honey.

JODY. Mama, can't I stay up just a little while and listen to the radio.

BERTHA. (*offstage*) Jody, you heard me.

JODY. But Mama, I don't wanna stay up all night. Just half an hour.

BERTHA. (*offstage*) Jody!

JODY. All right, Mama.

BERTHA. (*offstage*) And honey, I don't want you comin' downstairs in the middle of the night, sleeping on the couch and leaving the radio on all night.

JODY. All right, Mama.

BERTHA. (*offstage*) Good night, honey.

JODY. Good night.

JODY AS PUPPY. (*whine*)

JODY. Shhhh. You're gonna get us into hot water.

PUPPY. (*whine*)

BERTHA. (*offstage*) Jody, honey, the puppy is whining!

JODY. I'm taking care of it, Mama.

BERTHA. (*offstage*) Jody, put the puppy out now.

JODY. All right, Mama.

BERTHA. (*offstage*) And say your prayers.

JODY. I will, Mama. (*pause*)

BERTHA. (*offstage*) I'm listening!

JODY. Dear God, thank you for the puppy . . . and thank you for summer vacation . . . and God bless Mama. Amen. (*HE starts upstairs with puppy.*)

BERTHA. (*offstage*) And leave the puppy outside!

PUPPY. (*whine; JODY puts the puppy out and exits, and changes to CHARLENE. BERTHA enters.*)

BERTHA. Went out to check on the hired hands, huh? Well, that's a new one. I bet he spent a long time thinkin' that one up. Oh, Lord, Lord, I need help. I need strength, Lord. As you know, last week I bought a gun. And Lord, you have just got to give me strength not to buy any bullets. Amen.

(*MUSIC. BERTHA exits and changes to R.R. CHARLENE enters.*)

CHARLENE. Come on y'all, yell:
Two bits, four bits . . .

BERTHA. (*offstage*) Charlene, remember that promise we made. You promised if you didn't get cheerleader, you'd quit that practicing. So quit!

CHARLENE. All right, Mother.

BERTHA. (*offstage*) Goodnight, baby. Say your prayers.

CHARLENE. I don't even know why I'm talking to you. The way I look at it, I've had seven years, three in Junior High and four in High School to get cheerleader. I've prayed to you 'til my knees are flat, and nothin'. Well, I'm givin' notice. I'm becoming an official agnostic. Try that on! . . . Amen. (*CHARLENE exits and changes to DIDI. R.R. enters, playing fiddle.*)

DIDI. (*offstage*) R.R.? . . . R.R., where in the hell are you? (*enters*) R.R.?

R.R. I swear I saw it, Didi.

DIDI. Sure you did, R.R. You saw that hovering chalupa. You and Mogen David.

R.R. Now Didi, I wasn't drinkin' when . . .

DIDI. (*interrupts*) Shut up! Goddammit, I swear to God, if Mama was dead and I wasn't such a hard-shell Baptist, I swear to God I'd divorce your ass.

(*DIDI exits and changes to PETEY. R.R. starts to fiddle when a UFO appears. The UFO flies off; R.R. shrugs and exits, fiddling, and changes to ELMER. We hear ON TAPE:*)

THURSTON. (*tape*) Good evening, Tuna. This is Thurston Wheelis.

ARLES. (*tape*) And this is Arles Struvie.

THURSTON. (*tape*) And this is the Wheelis-

ARLES. (*tape*) Struvie-

THURSTON. (*tape*) Bedtime Report. And now for the news, take it away, Arles.

ARLES. (*tape*) Well, actually, we had a lot of news, but we lost it. We did.

THURSTON. (*tape*) We did?

ARLES. (*tape*) We did. We did.

THURSTON. (*tape*) Well, did you look under the table?

ARLES. (*tape*) I've looked everywhere . . . and I can't find it, but we'll be back in a minute and we'll find it and we'll have it for you.

THURSTON. (*tape*) Well, did you look over here?

ARLES. (*tape*) Well, I . . . Where in the hell did I put that thing? (*ELMER enters.*)

ELMER. All right, everybody, settle down. Let's begin this meetin'. First, let's bow our heads in a word of prayer. Lord, we just wanted to drop you a line to let you know we're still dedicated to doing your work, and that we still believe in making this world a better place for the right kind of people. Amen. (*ELMER starts to exit.*)

ELMER as YIPPY. Yip yip (*ELMER exits and changes to THURSTON; PETEY enters.*)

PETEY. Listen . . .

YIPPY. (*offstage*) Yip yip

PETEY. Listen, here it is: "Any animal that can't be adopted within a reasonable amount of time must be destroyed at state expense. Destroying the animal is the only humane recourse." Now, Yippy, you can't say I haven't tried. You've been pet-of-the-week five times, and that's a record, and I'd love to keep you. But I got to stop somewhere. It's getting crowded here with the animals I already got, and the ducks are just starting to arrive . . . You stop it. Now I mean it, you just quit that . . . How can I put you out of your misery if you're wagging your tail . . . (*pause*) Come on . . . All right. You got me. You can stay. Come on. Come on, go on out there in the back yard and play.

YIPPY. (*offstage*) Yip yip yip yip yip

PETEY. Hey, hey, don't bark at Ruth. Snakes are very sensitive . . . I don't know if there's anybody up there. I never have understood much about religion, but if you are, I'd like to ask a few favors for the animals. Now I'm doing the best I can, but I've got two dozen dogs, and I don't even have a count on the cats, and of course, there's Ruth, and the ducks, and Yippy. And the other thing is huntin' season is just around the corner and that means the nightmares are gonna start again. Now after I hear the first shot, the nightmares start and they don't stop 'til November. I hate to bother you with it. I really do. But if you are up there and if you did create all this, we could sure use some help takin' care of it. Thank you. Amen. (*PETEY starts to exit.*)

PETEY as ARLES. Hell, it's gotta be here somewhere. (*PETEY exits and changes to ARLES, as THURSTON enters.*)

THURSTON. Well, did you look in the car?

ARLES. (*offstage*) Yeah.

THURSTON. Well, did you look in the icebox?

ARLES. (*offstage*) Hell, I've looked everywhere, and I can't find it.

THURSTON. Well, I'd look out back in the trash . . . (*ARLES enters.*)

ARLES. Well, folks, I tell you, we've lost the news.

THURSTON. We have.

ARLES. We have. We have. I give up, Coach, take me out. I can't find the news. (*THEY laugh.*) So we're gonna say good night to ya . . .

THURSTON. Good night!

ARLES. . . . And we'll see you tomorrow.

THURSTON. See you tomorrow.

ARLES. 'Til then, remember our motto here at Radio OKKK: If you can find someplace you like better than Tuna . . .

ARLES & THURSTON. MOVE!

(*We hear the first three bars of "The Star Spangled Banner", then segue to; EXIT MUSIC.*)

END OF ACT II

COSTUME PLOT

ARLES
- green work pants
- rust print western shirt
- casual loafers
- white socks
- light brown belt
- mustache
- straw cowboy hat

THURSTON
- worn denim overalls
- red plaid flannel shirt
- black loafers
- glasses

DIDI
- red and white plastic raincoat
- red print scarf with curly bangs sewn in front
- white ankle socks
- slippers with a little heel

HAROLD DEAN
- yellow storm coat
- red umbrella

ELMER
- blue windbreaker
- black baseball cap (with rifle association patch)
- (worn over Thurston)

PETEY
- blue denim work jacket
- grey wool cap with flaps that cover the ears
  - (signs on cap change with each entrance—"save the scorpions", "save the whales", "save the scallops", etc.)

(worn over Arles except in scene with Bertha
and Yippy he wears Phinas' pants and shoes.)

BERTHA
lime green polyester pants suit
orange print arnel blouse
blue house slippers
glasses and chain
earrings
apron
bouffant wig
ACT II
green and red print flannel robe
hair clips

JODY
cut-off overalls
green and white striped tee shirt
orange baseball cap
cowboy boots
ACT II
cotton pajama bottoms
Snoopy tee shirt

STANLEY
green army pants
Zig Zag tee shirt
red bandana headband
sandals

CHARLENE
blue jeans with red sash belt
pink print top with ruffle collar
sneakers with pink pompoms
ponytail wraps with pink pompoms
glasses
ACT II
pink print pajamas

CHAD HARTFORD
  white linen pants
  orange Hawaiian shirt
  brown loafers
  sunglasses
  coke spoon on a long gold chain
  shoulder bag
  brown belt
LEONARD
  3 piece blue western suit with floral yoke
  white shirt with silver tips on collar
  string tie with turquoise pull
  white patent leather shoes
  grey/white wig
  glasses
PHINAS
  dark grey suit
  white shirt
  black tie shoes
  grey tie
  glasses
  dark brown wig
PEARL
  old lady's blue print dress
  beads that look like pearls
  pearl cluster earrings
  old lady black shoes
  cotton stockings
  little blue hat with veil
  cane
  glasses
  white gloves
  black purse with handkerchief and other
    paraphernalia

ACT II
  chenille robe
  hair net
VERA
  peach polyester dress
  white shoes
  white pillbox hat
  white lace gloves
  white glasses
  blonde wig
R.R. SNAVELY
  madras sports jacket
  straw hat
    (worn over Thurston)
REV. SPIKES
  3 piece white suit
  white shirt
  black ribbon tie
  straw panama hat
  glasses
  gold lapel pins
  mustache
SHERIFF
  brown on brown uniform
  brown cowboy hat
  gun and holster on leather belt
  cowboy boots
  sunglasses
  insignias on shirt (Tuna, Texas, an American flag,
    badge, etc.)
HANK
  blue jeans
  western shirt
  boots (same as sheriff)
  straw cowboy hat

Note—Where no shoes are indicated, Arles' or Thurston's are worn. Padding is built in as needed. All costumes are specially rigged for fast changes.

PROPERTY LIST

FURNITURE
    2 kitchen tables (formica and chrome)
    4 kitchen chairs (2 vinyl, 2 wood)
    an old fashioned cabinet floor model radio
SET DRESSING
    3 coat racks with various pieces of clothing
SIGNS
    ON THE AIR — practical

All of the following are practical and light at nightfall:
    FIRESTONE
    SEALTEST — Ray Hubbs
    MOTOROLA
    ICE CUBES
    LONE STAR BEER
    COCA COLA
    SEVEN UP BOTTLE
    NEON — MILLER HIGH LIFE BEER, MOTEL
PROPS — all props are mimed except
    knife (Bertha)
    National Enquirer (Bertha)
    gun and holster (Sheriff)